Oliver Wendell Holmes

The Poetical Works
Volume 2

Oliver Wendell Holmes

The Poetical Works
Volume 2

1st Edition | ISBN: 978-3-75230-307-0

Place of Publication: Frankfurt am Main, Germany

Year of Publication: 2020

Outlook Verlag GmbH, Germany.

Reproduction of the original.

THE POETICAL WORKS

OF

OLIVER WENDELL HOLMES

[Volume 2 of the 1893 three volume set]

THE CHAMBERED NAUTILUS

THIS is the ship of pearl, which, poets feign,
Sails the unshadowed main,—
The venturous bark that flings
On the sweet summer wind its purpled wings
In gulfs enchanted, where the Siren sings,
And coral reefs lie bare,
Where the cold sea-maids rise to sun their streaming hair.

Its webs of living gauze no more unfurl;
Wrecked is the ship of pearl!
And every chambered cell,
Where its dim dreaming life was wont to dwell,
As the frail tenant shaped his growing shell,
Before thee lies revealed,—
Its irised ceiling rent, its sunless crypt unsealed!

Year after year beheld the silent toil
That spread his lustrous coil;
Still, as the spiral grew,
He left the past year's dwelling for the new,
Stole with soft step its shining archway through,
Built up its idle door,
Stretched in his last-found home, and knew the old no more.

Thanks for the heavenly message brought by thee,
Child of the wandering sea,
Cast from her lap, forlorn!
From thy dead lips a clearer note is born
Than ever Triton blew from wreathed horn
While on mine ear it rings,
Through the deep caves of thought I hear a voice that sings:—

Build thee more stately mansions, O my soul,
As the swift seasons roll!
Leave thy low-vaulted past!
Let each new temple, nobler than the last,
Shut thee from heaven with a dome more vast,
Till thou at length art free;
Leaving thine outgrown shell by life's unresting sea!

SUN AND SHADOW

As I look from the isle, o'er its billows of green,
To the billows of foam-crested blue,
Yon bark, that afar in the distance is seen,
Half dreaming, my eyes will pursue
Now dark in the shadow, she scatters the spray
As the chaff in the stroke of the flail;
Now white as the sea-gull, she flies on her way,
The sun gleaming bright on her sail.

Yet her pilot is thinking of dangers to shun,—
Of breakers that whiten and roar;
How little he cares, if in shadow or sun
They see him who gaze from the shore!
He looks to the beacon that looms from the reef,
To the rock that is under his lee,
As he drifts on the blast, like a wind-wafted leaf,
O'er the gulfs of the desolate sea.

Thus drifting afar to the dim-vaulted caves
Where life and its ventures are laid,
The dreamers who gaze while we battle the waves
May see us in sunshine or shade;
Yet true to our course, though the shadows grow dark,
We'll trim our broad sail as before,
And stand by the rudder that governs the bark,
Nor ask how we look from the shore!

MUSA

O MY lost beauty!—hast thou folded quite

Thy wings of morning light
Beyond those iron gates
Where Life crowds hurrying to the haggard Fates,
And Age upon his mound of ashes waits
To chill our fiery dreams,
Hot from the heart of youth plunged in his icy streams?

Leave me not fading in these weeds of care,
Whose flowers are silvered hair!
Have I not loved thee long,
Though my young lips have often done thee wrong,
And vexed thy heaven-tuned ear with careless song?
Ah, wilt thou yet return,
Bearing thy rose-hued torch, and bid thine altar burn?

Come to me!—I will flood thy silent shrine
With my soul's sacred wine,
And heap thy marble floors
As the wild spice-trees waste their fragrant stores,
In leafy islands walled with madrepores
And lapped in Orient seas,
When all their feathery palms toss, plume-like, in the breeze.

Come to me!—thou shalt feed on honeyed words,
Sweeter than song of birds;—
No wailing bulbul's throat,
No melting dulcimer's melodious note
When o'er the midnight wave its murmurs float,
Thy ravished sense might soothe
With flow so liquid-soft, with strain so velvet-smooth.

Thou shalt be decked with jewels, like a queen,
Sought in those bowers of green
Where loop the clustered vines
And the close-clinging dulcamara twines,—
Pure pearls of Maydew where the moonlight shines,
And Summer's fruited gems,
And coral pendants shorn from Autumn's berried stems.

Sit by me drifting on the sleepy waves,—
Or stretched by grass-grown graves,
Whose gray, high-shouldered stones,
Carved with old names Life's time-worn roll disowns,
Lean, lichen-spotted, o'er the crumbled bones
Still slumbering where they lay
While the sad Pilgrim watched to scare the wolf away.

Spread o'er my couch thy visionary wing!
Still let me dream and sing,—
Dream of that winding shore
Where scarlet cardinals bloom-for me no more,—
The stream with heaven beneath its liquid floor,

And clustering nenuphars
Sprinkling its mirrored blue like golden-chaliced stars!

Come while their balms the linden-blossoms shed!—
Come while the rose is red,—
While blue-eyed Summer smiles
On the green ripples round yon sunken piles
Washed by the moon-wave warm from Indian isles,
And on the sultry air
The chestnuts spread their palms like holy men in prayer!

Oh for thy burning lips to fire my brain
With thrills of wild, sweet pain!—
On life's autumnal blast,
Like shrivelled leaves, youth's passion-flowers are cast,—
Once loving thee, we love thee to the last!—
Behold thy new-decked shrine,
And hear once more the voice that breathed "Forever thine!"

A PARTING HEALTH

TO J. L. MOTLEY

YES, we knew we must lose him,—though friendship may claim
To blend her green leaves with the laurels of fame;
Though fondly, at parting, we call him our own,
'T is the whisper of love when the bugle has blown.

As the rider that rests with the spur on his heel,
As the guardsman that sleeps in his corselet of steel,
As the archer that stands with his shaft on the string,
He stoops from his toil to the garland we bring.

What pictures yet slumber unborn in his loom,
Till their warriors shall breathe and their beauties shall bloom,

While the tapestry lengthens the life-glowing dyes
That caught from our sunsets the stain of their skies!

In the alcoves of death, in the charnels of timid,
Where flit the gaunt spectres of passion and crime,
There are triumphs untold, there are martyrs unsung,
There are heroes yet silent to speak with his tongue!

Let us hear the proud story which time has bequeathed!
From lips that are warm with the freedom they breathed!
Let him summon its tyrants, and tell us their doom,
Though he sweep the black past like Van Tromp with his broom!

… … … … …

The dream flashes by, for the west-winds awake
On pampas, on prairie, o'er mountain and lake,
To bathe the swift bark, like a sea-girdled shrine,
With incense they stole from the rose and the pine.

So fill a bright cup with the sunlight that gushed
When the dead summer's jewels were trampled and crushed:
THE TRUE KNIGHT OF LEARNING,—the world holds him dear,—
Love bless him, Joy crown him, God speed his career!

1857.

WHAT WE ALL THINK

THAT age was older once than now,
In spite of locks untimely shed,
Or silvered on the youthful brow;
That babes make love and children wed.

That sunshine had a heavenly glow,
Which faded with those "good old days"
When winters came with deeper snow,

And autumns with a softer haze.

That—mother, sister, wife, or child—
The "best of women" each has known.
Were school-boys ever half so wild?
How young the grandpapas have grown!

That but for this our souls were free,
And but for that our lives were blest;
That in some season yet to be
Our cares will leave us time to rest.

Whene'er we groan with ache or pain,—
Some common ailment of the race,—
Though doctors think the matter plain,—
That ours is "a peculiar case."

That when like babes with fingers burned
We count one bitter maxim more,
Our lesson all the world has learned,
And men are wiser than before.

That when we sob o'er fancied woes,
The angels hovering overhead
Count every pitying drop that flows,
And love us for the tears we shed.

That when we stand with tearless eye
And turn the beggar from our door,
They still approve us when we sigh,
"Ah, had I but one thousand more!"

Though temples crowd the crumbled brink
O'erhanging truth's eternal flow,
Their tablets bold with what we think,
Their echoes dumb to what we know;

That one unquestioned text we read,
All doubt beyond, all fear above,
Nor crackling pile nor cursing creed
Can burn or blot it: GOD IS LOVE!

SPRING HAS COME

THE sunbeams, lost for half a year,
Slant through my pane their morning rays;
For dry northwesters cold and clear,
The east blows in its thin blue haze.

And first the snowdrop's bells are seen,
Then close against the sheltering wall
The tulip's horn of dusky green,
The peony's dark unfolding ball.

The golden-chaliced crocus burns;
The long narcissus-blades appear;
The cone-beaked hyacinth returns
To light her blue-flamed chandelier.

The willow's whistling lashes, wrung
By the wild winds of gusty March,
With sallow leaflets lightly strung,
Are swaying by the tufted larch.

The elms have robed their slender spray
With full-blown flower and embryo leaf;
Wide o'er the clasping arch of day
Soars like a cloud their hoary chief.

See the proud tulip's flaunting cup,
That flames in glory for an hour,—
Behold it withering,—then look up,—
How meek the forest monarch's flower!

When wake the violets, Winter dies;
When sprout the elm-buds, Spring is near:
When lilacs blossom, Summer cries,
"Bud, little roses! Spring is here!"

The windows blush with fresh bouquets,
Cut with the May-dew on their lips;
The radish all its bloom displays,
Pink as Aurora's finger-tips.

Nor less the flood of light that showers

On beauty's changed corolla-shades,—
The walks are gay as bridal bowers
With rows of many-petalled maids.

The scarlet shell-fish click and clash
In the blue barrow where they slide;
The horseman, proud of streak and splash,
Creeps homeward from his morning ride.

Here comes the dealer's awkward string,
With neck in rope and tail in knot,—
Rough colts, with careless country-swing,
In lazy walk or slouching trot.

… … … … . .

Wild filly from the mountain-side,
Doomed to the close and chafing thills,
Lend me thy long, untiring stride
To seek with thee thy western hills!

I hear the whispering voice of Spring,
The thrush's trill, the robin's cry,
Like some poor bird with prisoned wing
That sits and sings, but longs to fly.

Oh for one spot of living greed,—
One little spot where leaves can grow,—
To love unblamed, to walk unseen,
To dream above, to sleep below!

PROLOGUE

A PROLOGUE? Well, of course the ladies know,—
I have my doubts. No matter,—here we go!
What is a Prologue? Let our Tutor teach:
Pro means beforehand; logos stands for speech.
'T is like the harper's prelude on the strings,
The prima donna's courtesy ere she sings;
Prologues in metre are to other pros
As worsted stockings are to engine-hose.
"The world's a stage,"—as Shakespeare said, one day;
The stage a world—was what he meant to say.
The outside world's a blunder, that is clear;
The real world that Nature meant is here.
Here every foundling finds its lost mamma;
Each rogue, repentant, melts his stern papa;
Misers relent, the spendthrift's debts are paid,
The cheats are taken in the traps they laid;
One after one the troubles all are past
Till the fifth act comes right side up at last,
When the young couple, old folks, rogues, and all,
Join hands, so happy at the curtain's fall.
Here suffering virtue ever finds relief,
And black-browed ruffians always come to grief.
When the lorn damsel, with a frantic screech,
And cheeks as hueless as a brandy-peach,
Cries, "Help, kyind Heaven!" and drops upon her knees
On the green—baize,—beneath the (canvas) trees,—
See to her side avenging Valor fly:—
"Ha! Villain! Draw! Now, Terraitorr, yield or die!"

When the poor hero flounders in despair,
Some dear lost uncle turns up millionaire,
Clasps the young scapegrace with paternal joy,
Sobs on his neck, "My boy! MY BOY!! *MY BOY*!!!"

Ours, then, sweet friends, the real world to-night,
Of love that conquers in disaster's spite.
Ladies, attend! While woful cares and doubt
Wrong the soft passion in the world without,
Though fortune scowl, though prudence interfere,
One thing is certain: Love will triumph here!
Lords of creation, whom your ladies rule,—
The world's great masters, when you 're out of school,—
Learn the brief moral of our evening's play
Man has his will,—but woman has her way!
While man's dull spirit toils in smoke and fire,
Woman's swift instinct threads the electric wire,—
The magic bracelet stretched beneath the waves
Beats the black giant with his score of slaves.
All earthly powers confess your sovereign art
But that one rebel,—woman's wilful heart.
All foes you master, but a woman's wit
Lets daylight through you ere you know you 're hit.
So, just to picture what her art can do,
Hear an old story, made as good as new.

Rudolph, professor of the headsman's trade,
Alike was famous for his arm and blade.
One day a prisoner Justice had to kill
Knelt at the block to test the artist's skill.
Bare-armed, swart-visaged, gaunt, and shaggy-browed,
Rudolph the headsman rose above the crowd.
His falchion lighted with a sudden gleam,
As the pike's armor flashes in the stream.
He sheathed his blade; he turned as if to go;
The victim knelt, still waiting for the blow.
"Why strikest not? Perform thy murderous act,"
The prisoner said. (His voice was slightly cracked.)
"Friend, I have struck," the artist straight replied;
"Wait but one moment, and yourself decide."
He held his snuff-box,—"Now then, if you please!"
The prisoner sniffed, and, with a crashing sneeze,
Off his head tumbled,—bowled along the floor,—

Bounced down the steps;—the prisoner said no more!
Woman! thy falchion is a glittering eye;
If death lurk in it, oh how sweet to die!
Thou takest hearts as Rudolph took the head;
We die with love, and never dream we're dead!

LATTER-DAY WARNINGS

WHEN legislators keep the law,
When banks dispense with bolts and looks,
When berries—whortle, rasp, and straw—
Grow bigger downwards through the box,—

When he that selleth house or land
Shows leak in roof or flaw in right,—
When haberdashers choose the stand
Whose window hath the broadest light,—

When preachers tell us all they think,
And party leaders all they mean,—
When what we pay for, that we drink,
From real grape and coffee-bean,—

When lawyers take what they would give,
And doctors give what they would take,—
When city fathers eat to live,
Save when they fast for conscience' sake,—

When one that hath a horse on sale
Shall bring his merit to the proof,
Without a lie for every nail
That holds the iron on the hoof,—

When in the usual place for rips

Our gloves are stitched with special care,
And guarded well the whalebone tips
Where first umbrellas need repair,—

When Cuba's weeds have quite forgot
The power of suction to resist,
And claret-bottles harbor not
Such dimples as would hold your fist,—

When publishers no longer steal,
And pay for what they stole before,—
When the first locomotive's wheel
Rolls through the Hoosac Tunnel's bore;—

Till then let Cumming blaze away,
And Miller's saints blow up the globe;
But when you see that blessed day,
Then order your ascension robe.

ALBUM VERSES

WHEN Eve had led her lord away,
And Cain had killed his brother,
The stars and flowers, the poets say,
Agreed with one another.

To cheat the cunning tempter's art,
And teach the race its duty,
By keeping on its wicked heart
Their eyes of light and beauty.

A million sleepless lids, they say,
Will be at least a warning;
And so the flowers would watch by day,
The stars from eve to morning.

On hill and prairie, field and lawn,
Their dewy eyes upturning,
The flowers still watch from reddening dawn
Till western skies are burning.

Alas! each hour of daylight tells
A tale of shame so crushing,
That some turn white as sea-bleached shells,
And some are always blushing.

But when the patient stars look down
On all their light discovers,
The traitor's smile, the murderer's frown,
The lips of lying lovers,

They try to shut their saddening eyes,
And in the vain endeavor
We see them twinkling in the skies,
And so they wink forever.

A GOOD TIME GOING!

BRAVE singer of the coming time,
Sweet minstrel of the joyous present,
Crowned with the noblest wreath of rhyme,
The holly-leaf of Ayrshire's peasant,
Good by! Good by!—Our hearts and hands,
Our lips in honest Saxon phrases,
Cry, God be with him, till he stands
His feet among the English daisies!

'T is here we part;—for other eyes
The busy deck, the fluttering streamer,
The dripping arms that plunge and rise,
The waves in foam, the ship in tremor,

The kerchiefs waving from the pier,
The cloudy pillar gliding o'er him,
The deep blue desert, lone and drear,
With heaven above and home before him!

His home!—the Western giant smiles,
And twirls the spotty globe to find it;
This little speck the British Isles?
'T is but a freckle,—never mind it!
He laughs, and all his prairies roll,
Each gurgling cataract roars and chuckles,
And ridges stretched from pole to pole
Heave till they crack their iron knuckles!

But Memory blushes at the sneer,
And Honor turns with frown defiant,
And Freedom, leaning on her spear,
Laughs louder than the laughing giant
"An islet is a world," she said,
"When glory with its dust has blended,
And Britain keeps her noble dead
Till earth and seas and skies are rended!"

Beneath each swinging forest-bough
Some arm as stout in death reposes,—
From wave-washed foot to heaven-kissed brow
Her valor's life-blood runs in roses;
Nay, let our brothers of the West
Write smiling in their florid pages,
One half her soil has walked the rest
In poets, heroes, martyrs, sages!

Hugged in the clinging billow's clasp,
From sea-weed fringe to mountain heather,
The British oak with rooted grasp
Her slender handful holds together;—
With cliffs of white and bowers of green,
And Ocean narrowing to caress her,
And hills and threaded streams between,—
Our little mother isle, God bless her!

In earth's broad temple where we stand,
Fanned by the eastern gales that brought us,
We hold the missal in our hand,
Bright with the lines our Mother taught us.

Where'er its blazoned page betrays
The glistening links of gilded fetters,
Behold, the half-turned leaf displays
Her rubric stained in crimson letters!

Enough! To speed a parting friend
'T is vain alike to speak and listen;—
Yet stay,—these feeble accents blend
With rays of light from eyes that glisten.
Good by! once more,—and kindly tell
In words of peace the young world's story,—
And say, besides, we love too well
Our mothers' soil, our fathers' glory.

THE LAST BLOSSOM

THOUGH young no more, we still would dream
Of beauty's dear deluding wiles;
The leagues of life to graybeards seem
Shorter than boyhood's lingering miles.

Who knows a woman's wild caprice?
'It played with Goethe's silvered hair,
And many a Holy Father's "niece"
Has softly smoothed the papal chair.

When sixty bids us sigh in vain
To melt the heart of sweet sixteen,
We think upon those ladies twain
Who loved so well the tough old Dean.

We see the Patriarch's wintry face,
The maid of Egypt's dusky glow,
And dream that Youth and Age embrace,
As April violets fill with snow.

Tranced in her lord's Olympian smile
His lotus-loving Memphian lies,—
The musky daughter of the Nile,
With plaited hair and almond eyes.

Might we but share one wild caress
Ere life's autumnal blossoms fall,
And Earth's brown, clinging lips impress
The long cold kiss that waits us all!

My bosom heaves, remembering yet
The morning of that blissful day,
When Rose, the flower of spring, I met,
And gave my raptured soul away.

Flung from her eyes of purest blue,
A lasso, with its leaping chain,
Light as a loop of larkspurs, flew
O'er sense and spirit, heart and brain.

Thou com'st to cheer my waning age,
Sweet vision, waited for so long!
Dove that would seek the poet's cage
Lured by the magic breath of song!

She blushes! Ah, reluctant maid,
Love's drapeau rouge the truth has told!
O' er girlhood's yielding barricade
Floats the great Leveller's crimson fold!

Come to my arms!—love heeds not years;
No frost the bud of passion knows.
Ha! what is this my frenzy hears?
A voice behind me uttered,—Rose!

Sweet was her smile,—but not for me;
Alas! when woman looks too kind,
Just turn your foolish head and see,—
Some youth is walking close behind!

CONTENTMENT

"Man wants but little here below"

LITTLE I ask; my wants are few;
I only wish a hut of stone,
(A *very plain* brown stone will do,)
That I may call my own;—
And close at hand is such a one,
In yonder street that fronts the sun.

Plain food is quite enough for me;
Three courses are as good as ten;—
If Nature can subsist on three,
Thank Heaven for three. Amen
I always thought cold victual nice;—
My *choice* would be vanilla-ice.

I care not much for gold or land;—
Give me a mortgage here and there,—
Some good bank-stock, some note of hand,
Or trifling railroad share,—
I only ask that Fortune send
A *little* more than I shall spend.

Honors are silly toys, I know,
And titles are but empty names;
I would, *perhaps*, be Plenipo,—
But only near St. James;
I'm very sure I should not care
To fill our Gubernator's chair.

Jewels are baubles; 't is a sin
To care for such unfruitful things;—
One good-sized diamond in a pin,—
Some, not so large, in rings,—
A ruby, and a pearl, or so,
Will do for me;—I laugh at show.

My dame should dress in cheap attire;
(Good, heavy silks are never dear;)—
I own perhaps I might desire
Some shawls of true Cashmere,—
Some marrowy crapes of China silk,

19

Like wrinkled skins on scalded milk.

I would not have the horse I drive
So fast that folks must stop and stare;
An easy gait—two, forty-five—
Suits me; I do not care;—
Perhaps, for just a *single spurt*,
Some seconds less would do no hurt.

Of pictures, I should like to own
Titians and Raphaels three or four,—
I love so much their style and tone,
One Turner, and no more,
(A landscape,—foreground golden dirt,—
The sunshine painted with a squirt.)

Of books but few,—some fifty score
For daily use, and bound for wear;
The rest upon an upper floor;—
Some *little* luxury *there*
Of red morocco's gilded gleam
And vellum rich as country cream.

Busts, cameos, gems,—such things as these,
Which others often show for pride,
I value for their power to please,
And selfish churls deride;—
One Stradivarius, I confess,
Two Meerschaums, I would fain possess.

Wealth's wasteful tricks I will not learn,
Nor ape the glittering upstart fool;—
Shall not carved tables serve my turn,
But *all* must be of buhl?
Give grasping pomp its double share,—
I ask but *one* recumbent chair.

Thus humble let me live and die,
Nor long for Midas' golden touch;
If Heaven more generous gifts deny,
I shall not miss them much,—
Too grateful for the blessing lent
Of simple tastes and mind content!

AESTIVATION

AN UNPUBLISHED POEM, BY MY LATE LATIN TUTOR

IN candent ire the solar splendor flames;
The foles, langueseent, pend from arid rames;
His humid front the Give, anheling, wipes,
And dreams of erring on ventiferous riper.

How dulce to vive occult to mortal eyes,
Dorm on the herb with none to supervise,
Carp the suave berries from the crescent vine,
And bibe the flow from longicaudate kine!

To me, alas! no verdurous visions come,
Save yon exiguous pool's conferva-scum,—
No concave vast repeats the tender hue
That laves my milk-jug with celestial blue!

Me wretched! Let me curr to quercine shades!
Effund your albid hausts, lactiferous maids!
Oh, might I vole to some umbrageous clump,—
Depart,—be off,—excede,—evade,—erump!

THE DEACON'S MASTERPIECE

OR, THE WONDERFUL "ONE-HOSS SHAY"

A LOGICAL STORY

HAVE you heard of the wonderful one-hoss shay,
That was built in such a logical way
It ran a hundred years to a day,
And then, of a sudden, it—ah, but stay,

I 'll tell you what happened without delay,
Scaring the parson into fits,
Frightening people out of their wits,—
Have you ever heard of that, I say?

Seventeen hundred and fifty-five.
Georgius Secundus was then alive,—
Snuffy old drone from the German hive.
That was the year when Lisbon-town
Saw the earth open and gulp her down,
And Braddock's army was done so brown,
Left without a scalp to its crown.
It was on the terrible Earthquake-day
That the Deacon finished the one-hoss shay.

Now in building of chaises, I tell you what,
There is always *somewhere* a weakest spot,—
In hub, tire, felloe, in spring or thill,
In panel, or crossbar, or floor, or sill,
In screw, bolt, thoroughbrace,—lurking still,
Find it somewhere you must and will,—
Above or below, or within or without,—
And that 's the reason, beyond a doubt,
That a chaise breaks down, but does n't wear out.

But the Deacon swore (as Deacons do,
With an "I dew vum," or an "I tell yeou ")
He would build one shay to beat the taown
'n' the keounty 'n' all the kentry raoun';
It should be so built that it couldn' break daown
"Fur," said the Deacon, "'t 's mighty plain
Thut the weakes' place mus' stan' the strain;
'n' the way t' fix it, uz I maintain,
    Is only jest
T' make that place uz strong uz the rest."

So the Deacon inquired of the village folk
Where he could find the strongest oak,
That couldn't be split nor bent nor broke,—
That was for spokes and floor and sills;
He sent for lancewood to make the thills;
The crossbars were ash, from the straightest trees,
The panels of white-wood, that cuts like cheese,
But lasts like iron for things like these;

The hubs of logs from the "Settler's ellum,"—
Last of its timber,—they could n't sell 'em,
Never an axe had seen their chips,
And the wedges flew from between their lips,
Their blunt ends frizzled like celery-tips;
Step and prop-iron, bolt and screw,
Spring, tire, axle, and linchpin too,
Steel of the finest, bright and blue;
Thoroughbrace bison-skin, thick and wide;
Boot, top, dasher, from tough old hide
Found in the pit when the tanner died.
That was the way he "put her through."
"There!" said the Deacon, "naow she 'll dew!"

Do! I tell you, I rather guess
She was a wonder, and nothing less!
Colts grew horses, beards turned gray,
Deacon and deaconess dropped away,
Children and grandchildren—where were they?
But there stood the stout old one-hoss shay
As fresh as on Lisbon-earthquake-day!

EIGHTEEN HUNDRED;—it came and found
The Deacon's masterpiece strong and sound.
Eighteen hundred increased by ten;—
"Hahnsum kerridge" they called it then.
Eighteen hundred and twenty came;—
Running as usual; much the same.
Thirty and forty at last arrive,
And then come fifty, and FIFTY-FIVE.
First of November, 'Fifty-five!
This morning the parson takes a drive.
Now, small boys, get out of the way!
Here comes the wonderful one-hoss shay,

Little of all we value here
Wakes on the morn of its hundredth year
Without both feeling and looking queer.
In fact, there 's nothing that keeps its youth,
So far as I know, but a tree and truth.
(This is a moral that runs at large;
Take it.—You 're welcome.—No extra charge.)

FIRST OF NOVEMBER,—the Earthquake-day,—

There are traces of age in the one-hoss shay,
A general flavor of mild decay,
But nothing local, as one may say.
There couldn't be,—for the Deacon's art
Had made it so like in every part
That there was n't a chance for one to start.
For the wheels were just as strong as the thills,
And the floor was just as strong as the sills,
And the panels just as strong as the floor,
And the whipple-tree neither less nor more,
And the back-crossbar as strong as the fore,
And spring and axle and hub encore.
And yet, as a whole, it is past a doubt
In another hour it will be worn out!

Drawn by a rat-tailed, ewe-necked bay.
"Huddup!" said the parson.—Off went they.
The parson was working his Sunday's text,—
Had got to fifthly, and stopped perplexed
At what the—Moses—was coming next.
All at once the horse stood still,
Close by the meet'n'-house on the hill.
First a shiver, and then a thrill,
Then something decidedly like a spill,—
And the parson was sitting upon a rock,
At half past nine by the meet'n'-house clock,—
Just the hour of the Earthquake shock!
What do you think the parson found,
When he got up and stared around?
The poor old chaise in a heap or mound,
As if it had been to the mill and ground!
You see, of course, if you 're not a dunce,
How it went to pieces all at once,—
All at once, and nothing first,—
Just as bubbles do when they burst.

End of the wonderful one-hoss shay.
Logic is logic. That's all I say.

PARSON TURELL'S LEGACY

OR, THE PRESIDENT'S OLD ARM-CHAIR

A MATHEMATICAL STORY

FACTS respecting an old arm-chair.
At Cambridge. Is kept in the College there.
Seems but little the worse for wear.
That 's remarkable when I say
It was old in President Holyoke's day.
(One of his boys, perhaps you know,
Died, *at one hundred*, years ago.)
He took lodgings for rain or shine
Under green bed-clothes in '69.

Know old Cambridge? Hope you do.—
Born there? Don't say so! I was, too.
(Born in a house with a gambrel-roof,—
Standing still, if you must have proof.—
"Gambrel?—Gambrel?"—Let me beg
You'll look at a horse's hinder leg,—
First great angle above the hoof,—
That 's the gambrel; hence gambrel-roof.)
Nicest place that ever was seen,—
Colleges red and Common green,
Sidewalks brownish with trees between.
Sweetest spot beneath the skies
When the canker-worms don't rise,—
When the dust, that sometimes flies
Into your mouth and ears and eyes,
In a quiet slumber lies,
Not in the shape of umbaked pies
Such as barefoot children prize.

A kind of harbor it seems to be,
Facing the flow of a boundless sea.
Rows of gray old Tutors stand
Ranged like rocks above the sand;
Rolling beneath them, soft and green,
Breaks the tide of bright sixteen,—

One wave, two waves, three waves, four,—
Sliding up the sparkling floor.

Then it ebbs to flow no more,
Wandering off from shore to shore
With its freight of golden ore!
Pleasant place for boys to play;—
Better keep your girls away;
Hearts get rolled as pebbles do
Which countless fingering waves pursue,
And every classic beach is strown
With heart-shaped pebbles of blood-red stone.

But this is neither here nor there;
I 've talking about an old arm-chair.
You 've heard, no doubt, of PARSON TURELL?
Over at Medford he used to dwell;
Married one of the Mathers' folk;
Got with his wife a chair of oak,—
Funny old chair with seat like wedge,
Sharp behind and broad front edge,—
One of the oddest of human things,
Turned all over with knobs and rings,—
But heavy, and wide, and deep, and grand,—
Fit for the worthies of the land,—
Chief Justice Sewall a cause to try in,
Or Cotton Mather to sit—and lie—in.
Parson Turell bequeathed the same
To a certain student,—SMITH by name;
These were the terms, as we are told:
"Saide Smith saide Chaire to have and holde;
When he doth graduate, then to passe
To ye oldest Youth in ye Senior Classe.
On payment of "—(naming a certain sum)—
"By him to whom ye Chaire shall come;
He to ye oldest Senior next,
And soe forever,"—(thus runs the text,)—
"But one Crown lesse then he gave to claime,
That being his Debte for use of same."
Smith transferred it to one of the BROWNS,
And took his money,—five silver crowns.
Brown delivered it up to MOORE,
Who paid, it is plain, not five, but four.

Moore made over the chair to LEE,
Who gave him crowns of silver three.
Lee conveyed it unto DREW,
And now the payment, of course, was two.
Drew gave up the chair to DUNN,—
All he got, as you see, was one.
Dunn released the chair to HALL,
And got by the bargain no crown at all.
And now it passed to a second BROWN,
Who took it and likewise claimed a crown.
When Brown conveyed it unto WARE,
Having had one crown, to make it fair,
He paid him two crowns to take the chair;
And Ware, being honest, (as all Wares be,)
He paid one POTTER, who took it, three.
Four got ROBINSON; five got Dix;
JOHNSON primus demanded six;
And so the sum kept gathering still
Till after the battle of Bunker's Hill.

When paper money became so cheap,
Folks would n't count it, but said "a heap,"
A certain RICHARDS,—the books declare,—
(A. M. in '90? I've looked with care
Through the Triennial,—name not there,)—
This person, Richards, was offered then
Eightscore pounds, but would have ten;
Nine, I think, was the sum he took,—
Not quite certain,—but see the book.
By and by the wars were still,
But nothing had altered the Parson's will.
The old arm-chair was solid yet,
But saddled with such a monstrous debt!
Things grew quite too bad to bear,
Paying such sums to get rid of the chair
But dead men's fingers hold awful tight,
And there was the will in black and white,
Plain enough for a child to spell.
What should be done no man could tell,
For the chair was a kind of nightmare curse,
And every season but made it worse.

As a last resort, to clear the doubt,

They got old GOVERNOR HANCOCK out.
The Governor came with his Lighthorse Troop
And his mounted truckmen, all cock-a-hoop;
Halberds glittered and colors flew,
French horns whinnied and trumpets blew,
The yellow fifes whistled between their teeth,
And the bumble-bee bass-drums boomed beneath;
So he rode with all his band,
Till the President met him, cap in hand.
The Governor "hefted" the crowns, and said,—
"A will is a will, and the Parson's dead."
The Governor hefted the crowns. Said he,—
"There is your p'int. And here 's my fee.

"These are the terms you must fulfil,—
On such conditions I BREAK THE WILL!"
The Governor mentioned what these should be.
(Just wait a minute and then you 'll see.)
The President prayed. Then all was still,
And the Governor rose and BROKE THE WILL!
"About those conditions?" Well, now you go
And do as I tell you, and then you'll know.
Once a year, on Commencement day,
If you 'll only take the pains to stay,
You'll see the President in the CHAIR,
Likewise the Governor sitting there.
The President rises; both old and young
May hear his speech in a foreign tongue,
The meaning whereof, as lawyers swear,
Is this: Can I keep this old arm-chair?
And then his Excellency bows,
As much as to say that he allows.
The Vice-Gub. next is called by name;
He bows like t' other, which means the same.
And all the officers round 'em bow,
As much as to say that they allow.
And a lot of parchments about the chair
Are handed to witnesses then and there,
And then the lawyers hold it clear
That the chair is safe for another year.

God bless you, Gentlemen! Learn to give
Money to colleges while you live.

Don't be silly and think you'll try
To bother the colleges, when you die,
With codicil this, and codicil that,
That Knowledge may starve while Law grows fat;
For there never was pitcher that wouldn't spill,
And there's always a flaw in a donkey's will!

ODE FOR A SOCIAL MEETING

WITH SLIGHT ALTERATIONS BY A TEETOTALER—(...)

COME! fill a fresh bumper, for why should we go
While the nectar (logwood) still reddens our cups as they flow?
Pour out the rich juices (decoction) still bright with the sun,
Till o'er the brimmed crystal the rubies (dye-stuff) shall run.

The purple-globed clusters (half-ripened apples) their life-dews have
    bled;
How sweet is the breath (taste) of the fragrance they shed!(sugar of
lead)
For summer's last roses (rank poisons) lie hid in the wines (wines!!!)
That were garnered by maidens who laughed through the vines (stable-boys
smoking long-nines)

Then a smile (scowl) and a glass (howl) and a toast (scoff) and a cheer
(sneer); For all the good wine, and we 've some of it here! (strychnine and
whiskey, and ratsbane and beer!) In cellar, in pantry, in attic, in hall, Long live
the gay servant that laughs for us all! (Down, down with the tyrant that
masters us all!)

POEMS FROM THE PROFESSOR AT THE BREAKFAST-TABLE

1858-1859

UNDER THE VIOLETS

HER hands are cold; her face is white;
No more her pulses come and go;

Her eyes are shut to life and light;—
Fold the white vesture, snow on snow,
And lay her where the violets blow.

But not beneath a graven stone,
To plead for tears with alien eyes;
A slender cross of wood alone
Shall say, that here a maiden lies
In peace beneath the peaceful skies.

And gray old trees of hugest limb
Shall wheel their circling shadows round
To make the scorching sunlight dim
That drinks the greenness from the ground,
And drop their dead leaves on her mound.

When o'er their boughs the squirrels run,
And through their leaves the robins call,
And, ripening in the autumn sun,
The acorns and the chestnuts fall,
Doubt not that she will heed them all.

For her the morning choir shall sing
Its matins from the branches high,
And every minstrel-voice of Spring,
That trills beneath the April sky,
Shall greet her with its earliest cry.

When, turning round their dial-track,
Eastward the lengthening shadows pass,
Her little mourners, clad in black,
The crickets, sliding through the grass,
Shall pipe for her an evening mass.

At last the rootlets of the trees
Shall find the prison where she lies,
And bear the buried dust they seize
In leaves and blossoms to the skies.
So may the soul that warmed it rise!

If any, born of kindlier blood,
Should ask, What maiden lies below?
Say only this: A tender bud,
That tried to blossom in the snow,
Lies withered where the violets blow.

HYMN OF TRUST

O Love Divine, that stooped to share
Our sharpest pang, our bitterest tear,
On Thee we cast each earth-born care,
We smile at pain while Thou art near!

Though long the weary way we tread,
And sorrow crown each lingering year,
No path we shun, no darkness dread,
Our hearts still whispering, Thou art near!

When drooping pleasure turns to grief,
And trembling faith is changed to fear,
The murmuring wind, the quivering leaf,
Shall softly tell us, Thou art near!

On Thee we fling our burdening woe,
O Love Divine, forever dear,
Content to suffer while we know,
Living and dying, Thou art near!

A SUN-DAY HYMN

LORD of all being! throned afar,
Thy glory flames from sun and star;
Centre and soul of every sphere,
Yet to each loving heart how near!

Sun of our life, thy quickening ray
Sheds on our path the glow of day;
Star of our hope, thy softened light
Cheers the long watches of the night.

Our midnight is thy smile withdrawn;
Our noontide is thy gracious dawn;
Our rainbow arch thy mercy's sign;
All, save the clouds of sin, are thin!

Lord of all life, below, above,
Whose light is truth, whose warmth is love,
Before thy ever-blazing throne
We ask no lustre of our own.

Grant us thy truth to make us free,
And kindling hearts that burn for thee,
Till all thy living altars claim
One holy light, one heavenly flame!

THE CROOKED FOOTPATH

AH, here it is! the sliding rail
That marks the old remembered spot,—
The gap that struck our school-boy trail,—
The crooked path across the lot.

It left the road by school and church,
A pencilled shadow, nothing more,
That parted from the silver-birch
And ended at the farm-house door.

No line or compass traced its plan;
With frequent bends to left or right,
In aimless, wayward curves it ran,
But always kept the door in sight.

The gabled porch, with woodbine green,—
The broken millstone at the sill,—
Though many a rood might stretch between,
The truant child could see them still.

No rocks across the pathway lie,—
No fallen trunk is o'er it thrown,—
And yet it winds, we know not why,
And turns as if for tree or stone.

Perhaps some lover trod the way
With shaking knees and leaping heart,—
And so it often runs astray
With sinuous sweep or sudden start.

Or one, perchance, with clouded brain
From some unholy banquet reeled,—
And since, our devious steps maintain
His track across the trodden field.

Nay, deem not thus,—no earthborn will
Could ever trace a faultless line;
Our truest steps are human still,—
To walk unswerving were divine!

Truants from love, we dream of wrath;
Oh, rather let us trust the more!
Through all the wanderings of the path,
We still can see our Father's door!

IRIS, HER BOOK

I PRAY thee by the soul of her that bore thee,
By thine own sister's spirit I implore thee,
Deal gently with the leaves that lie before thee!

For Iris had no mother to infold her,
Nor ever leaned upon a sister's shoulder,
Telling the twilight thoughts that Nature told her.

She had not learned the mystery of awaking

Those chorded keys that soothe a sorrow's aching,
Giving the dumb heart voice, that else were breaking.

Yet lived, wrought, suffered. Lo, the pictured token
Why should her fleeting day-dreams fade unspoken,
Like daffodils that die with sheaths unbroken?

She knew not love, yet lived in maiden fancies,—
Walked simply clad, a queen of high romances,
And talked strange tongues with angels in her trances.

Twin-souled she seemed, a twofold nature wearing:
Sometimes a flashing falcon in her daring,
Then a poor mateless dove that droops despairing.

Questioning all things: Why her Lord had sent her?
What were these torturing gifts, and wherefore lent her?
Scornful as spirit fallen, its own tormentor.

And then all tears and anguish: Queen of Heaven,
Sweet Saints, and Thou by mortal sorrows riven,
Save me! Oh, save me! Shall I die forgiven?

And then—Ah, God! But nay, it little matters:
Look at the wasted seeds that autumn scatters,
The myriad germs that Nature shapes and shatters!

If she had—Well! She longed, and knew not wherefore.
Had the world nothing she might live to care for?
No second self to say her evening prayer for?

She knew the marble shapes that set men dreaming,
Yet with her shoulders bare and tresses streaming
Showed not unlovely to her simple seeming.

Vain? Let it be so! Nature was her teacher.
What if a lonely and unsistered creature
Loved her own harmless gift of pleasing feature,

Saying, unsaddened,—This shall soon be faded,
And double-hued the shining tresses braided,
And all the sunlight of the morning shaded?

This her poor book is full of saddest follies,
Of tearful smiles and laughing melancholies,
With summer roses twined and wintry hollies.

In the strange crossing of uncertain chances,
Somewhere, beneath some maiden's tear-dimmed glances

May fall her little book of dreams and fancies.

Sweet sister! Iris, who shall never name thee,
Trembling for fear her open heart may shame thee,
Speaks from this vision-haunted page to claim thee.

Spare her, I pray thee! If the maid is sleeping,
Peace with her! she has had her hour of weeping.
No more! She leaves her memory in thy keeping.

ROBINSON OF LEYDEN

HE sleeps not here; in hope and prayer
His wandering flock had gone before,
But he, the shepherd, might not share
Their sorrows on the wintry shore.

Before the Speedwell's anchor swung,
Ere yet the Mayflower's sail was spread,
While round his feet the Pilgrims clung,
The pastor spake, and thus he said:—

"Men, brethren, sisters, children dear!
God calls you hence from over sea;
Ye may not build by Haerlem Meer,
Nor yet along the Zuyder-Zee.

"Ye go to bear the saving word
To tribes unnamed and shores untrod;
Heed well the lessons ye have heard
From those old teachers taught of God.

"Yet think not unto them was lent
All light for all the coming days,
And Heaven's eternal wisdom spent
In making straight the ancient ways;

"The living fountain overflows
For every flock, for every lamb,
Nor heeds, though angry creeds oppose
With Luther's dike or Calvin's dam."

He spake; with lingering, long embrace,
With tears of love and partings fond,
They floated down the creeping Maas,
Along the isle of Ysselmond.

They passed the frowning towers of Briel,
The "Hook of Holland's" shelf of sand,
And grated soon with lifting keel
The sullen shores of Fatherland.

No home for these!—too well they knew
The mitred king behind the throne;—
The sails were set, the pennons flew,
And westward ho! for worlds unknown.

And these were they who gave us birth,
The Pilgrims of the sunset wave,
Who won for us this virgin earth,
And freedom with the soil they gave.

The pastor slumbers by the Rhine,—
In alien earth the exiles lie,—
Their nameless graves our holiest shrine,
His words our noblest battle-cry!

Still cry them, and the world shall hear,
Ye dwellers by the storm-swept sea!
Ye *have* not built by Haerlem Meer,
Nor on the land-locked Zuyder-Zee!

ST. ANTHONY THE REFORMER

HIS TEMPTATION

No fear lest praise should make us proud!
We know how cheaply that is won;
The idle homage of the crowd
Is proof of tasks as idly done.

A surface-smile may pay the toil
That follows still the conquering Right,
With soft, white hands to dress the spoil
That sun-browned valor clutched in fight.

Sing the sweet song of other days,
Serenely placid, safely true,
And o'er the present's parching ways
The verse distils like evening dew.

But speak in words of living power,—
They fall like drops of scalding rain
That plashed before the burning shower
Swept o' er the cities of the plain!

Then scowling Hate turns deadly pale,—
Then Passion's half-coiled adders spring,
And, smitten through their leprous mail,
Strike right and left in hope to sting.

If thou, unmoved by poisoning wrath,
Thy feet on earth, thy heart above,
Canst walk in peace thy kingly path,
Unchanged in trust, unchilled in love,—

Too kind for bitter words to grieve,
Too firm for clamor to dismay,
When Faith forbids thee to believe,
And Meekness calls to disobey,—

Ah, then beware of mortal pride!
The smiling pride that calmly scorns
Those foolish fingers, crimson dyed
In laboring on thy crown of thorns!

THE OPENING OF THE PIANO

IN the little southern parlor of the house you may have seen
With the gambrel-roof, and the gable looking westward to the green,
At the side toward the sunset, with the window on its right,
Stood the London-made piano I am dreaming of to-night!

Ah me I how I remember the evening when it came!
What a cry of eager voices, what a group of cheeks in flame,
When the wondrous box was opened that had come from over seas,
With its smell of mastic-varnish and its flash of ivory keys!

Then the children all grew fretful in the restlessness of joy,
For the boy would push his sister, and the sister crowd the boy,
Till the father asked for quiet in his grave paternal way,
But the mother hushed the tumult with the words, "Now, Mary, play."

For the dear soul knew that music was a very sovereign balm;
She had sprinkled it over Sorrow and seen its brow grow calm,
In the days of slender harpsichords with tapping tinkling quills,
Or carolling to her spinet with its thin metallic thrills.

So Mary, the household minstrel, who always loved to please,
Sat down to the new "Clementi," and struck the glittering keys.
Hushed were the children's voices, and every eye grew dim,
As, floating from lip and finger, arose the "Vesper Hymn."

Catharine, child of a neighbor, curly and rosy-red,
(Wedded since, and a widow,—something like ten years dead,)
Hearing a gush of music such as none before,
Steals from her mother's chamber and peeps at the open door.

Just as the "Jubilate" in threaded whisper dies,
"Open it! open it, lady!" the little maiden cries,
(For she thought 't was a singing creature caged in a box she heard,)
"Open it! open it, lady! and let me see the *bird!*"

MIDSUMMER

HERE! sweep these foolish leaves away,
I will not crush my brains to-day!
Look! are the southern curtains drawn?
Fetch me a fan, and so begone!

Not that,—the palm-tree's rustling leaf
Brought from a parching coral-reef
Its breath is heated;—I would swing
The broad gray plumes,—the eagle's wing.

I hate these roses' feverish blood!
Pluck me a half-blown lily-bud,
A long-stemmed lily from the lake,
Cold as a coiling water-snake.

Rain me sweet odors on the air,
And wheel me up my Indian chair,
And spread some book not overwise
Flat out before my sleepy eyes.

Who knows it not,—this dead recoil
Of weary fibres stretched with toil,—
The pulse that flutters faint and low
When Summer's seething breezes blow!

O Nature! bare thy loving breast,
And give thy child one hour of rest,—
One little hour to lie unseen
Beneath thy scarf of leafy green!

So, curtained by a singing pine,
Its murmuring voice shall blend with mine,
Till, lost in dreams, my faltering lay
In sweeter music dies away.

DE SAUTY

AN ELECTRO-CHEMICAL ECLOGUE

The first messages received through the submarine cable were sent by an electrical expert, a mysterious personage who signed himself De Sauty.

Professor Blue-Nose

PROFESSOR
TELL me, O Provincial! speak, Ceruleo-Nasal!
Lives there one De Sauty extant now among you,
Whispering Boanerges, son of silent thunder,
Holding talk with nations?

Is there a De Sauty ambulant on Tellus,
Bifid-cleft like mortals, dormient in nightcap,
Having sight, smell, hearing, food-receiving feature
Three times daily patent?

Breathes there such a being, O Ceruleo-Nasal?
Or is he a *mythus*,—ancient word for "humbug"—
Such as Livy told about the wolf that wet-nursed
Romulus and Remus?

Was he born of woman, this alleged De Sauty?
Or a living product of galvanic action,
Like the acarus bred in Crosse's flint-solution?
Speak, thou Cyano-Rhinal!

BLUE-NOSE
Many things thou askest, jackknife-bearing stranger,
Much-conjecturing mortal, pork-and-treacle-waster!
Pretermit thy whittling, wheel thine ear-flap toward me,
Thou shall hear them answered.

When the charge galvanic tingled through the cable,
At the polar focus of the wire electric
Suddenly appeared a white-faced man among us
Called himself "DE SAUTY."

As the small opossum held in pouch maternal
Grasps the nutrient organ whence the term mammalia,
So the unknown stranger held the wire electric,
Sucking in the current.

When the current strengthened, bloomed the pale-faced stranger,—
Took no drink nor victual, yet grew fat and rosy,—
And from time to time, in sharp articulation,
Said, "All right! DE SAUTY."

From the lonely station passed the utterance, spreading
Through the pines and hemlocks to the groves of steeples,
Till the land was filled with loud reverberations
Of *"All right* DE SAUTY."

When the current slackened, drooped the mystic stranger,—
Faded, faded, faded, as the stream grew weaker,—
Wasted to a shadow, with a hartshorn odor
Of disintegration.

Drops of deliquescence glistened on his forehead,
Whitened round his feet the dust of efflorescence,
Till one Monday morning, when the flow suspended,
There was no De Sauty.

Nothing but a cloud of elements organic,
C. O. H. N. Ferrum, Chlor. Flu. Sil. Potassa,
Cale. Sod. Phosph. Mag. Sulphur, Mang. (?)
Alumin. (?) Cuprum, (?)
Such as man is made of.

Born of stream galvanic, with it he had perished!
There is no De Sauty now there is no current!
Give us a new cable, then again we'll hear him
Cry, "All right! DE SAUTY."

POEMS FROM THE POET AT THE BREAKFAST-TABLE

1871-1872

THE DIVINE VOICE
Go seek thine earth-born sisters,—thus the Voice
That all obey,—the sad and silent three;
These only, while the hosts of Heaven rejoice,
Smile never; ask them what their sorrows be;

And when the secret of their griefs they tell,
Look on them with thy mild, half-human eyes;
Say what thou wast on earth; thou knowest well;
So shall they cease from unavailing sighs.

THE ANGEL
Why thus, apart,—the swift-winged herald spake,—
Sit ye with silent lips and unstrung lyres
While the trisagion's blending chords awake
In shouts of joy from all the heavenly choirs?

FIRST SPIRIT
Chide not thy sisters,—thus the answer came;—
Children of earth, our half-weaned nature clings
To earth's fond memories, and her whispered name
Untunes our quivering lips, our saddened strings;

For there we loved, and where we love is home,
Home that our feet may leave, but not our hearts,
Though o'er us shine the jasper-lighted dome:—
The chain may lengthen, but it never parts!

Sometimes a sunlit sphere comes rolling by,
And then we softly whisper,—can it be?
And leaning toward the silvery orb, we try
To hear the music of its murmuring sea;

To catch, perchance, some flashing glimpse of green,
Or breathe some wild-wood fragrance, wafted through
The opening gates of pearl, that fold between
The blinding splendors and the changeless blue.

THE ANGEL
Nay, sister, nay! a single healing leaf
Plucked from the bough of yon twelve-fruited tree
Would soothe such anguish,—deeper stabbing grief

43

Has pierced thy throbbing heart—

THE FIRST SPIRIT
Ah, woe is me! I from my clinging babe was rudely torn;
His tender lips a loveless bosom pressed;
Can I forget him in my life new born?
Oh that my darling lay upon my breast!

THE ANGEL
And thou?—

THE SECOND SPIRIT
I was a fair and youthful bride,
The kiss of love still burns upon my cheek,
He whom I worshipped, ever at my side,—
Him through the spirit realm in vain I seek.

Sweet faces turn their beaming eyes on mine;
Ah! not in these the wished-for look I read;
Still for that one dear human smile I pine;
Thou and none other!—is the lover's creed.

THE ANGEL
And whence thy sadness in a world of bliss
Where never parting comes, nor mourner's tear?
Art thou, too, dreaming of a mortal's kiss
Amid the seraphs of the heavenly sphere?

THE THIRD SPIRIT
Nay, tax not me with passion's wasting fire;
When the swift message set my spirit free,
Blind, helpless, lone, I left my gray-haired sire;
My friends were many, he had none save me.

I left him, orphaned, in the starless night;
Alas, for him no cheerful morning's dawn
I wear the ransomed spirit's robe of white,
Yet still I hear him moaning, *She is gone!*

THE ANGEL
Ye know me not, sweet sisters?—All in vain
Ye seek your lost ones in the shapes they wore;
The flower once opened may not bud again,
The fruit once fallen finds the stem no more.

Child, lover, sire,—yea, all things loved below,—
Fair pictures damasked on a vapor's fold,—

Fade like the roseate flush, the golden glow,
When the bright curtain of the day is rolled.

I was the babe that slumbered on thy breast.
And, sister, mine the lips that called thee bride.
Mine were the silvered locks thy hand caressed,
That faithful hand, my faltering footstep's guide!

Each changing form, frail vesture of decay,
The soul unclad forgets it once hath worn,
Stained with the travel of the weary day,
And shamed with rents from every wayside
thorn.

To lie, an infant, in thy fond embrace,—
To come with love's warm kisses back to thee,—
To show thine eyes thy gray-haired father's face,
Not Heaven itself could grant; this may not be!

Then spread your folded wings, and leave to earth
The dust once breathing ye have mourned so long,
Till Love, new risen, owns his heavenly birth,
And sorrow's discords sweeten into song!

FANTASIA

THE YOUNG GIRL'S POEM

KISS mine eyelids, beauteous Morn,
Blushing into life new-born!
Lend me violets for my hair,
And thy russet robe to wear,
And thy ring of rosiest hue
Set in drops of diamond dew!

Kiss my cheek, thou noontide ray,

From my Love so far away
Let thy splendor streaming down
Turn its pallid lilies brown,
Till its darkening shades reveal
Where his passion pressed its seal!

Kiss my lips, thou Lord of light,
Kiss my lips a soft good-night!
Westward sinks thy golden car;
Leave me but the evening star,
And my solace that shall be,
Borrowing all its light from thee!

AUNT TABITHA

THE YOUNG GIRL'S POEM

WHATEVER I do, and whatever I say,
Aunt Tabitha tells me that is n't the way;
When she was a girl (forty summers ago)
Aunt Tabitha tells me they never did so.

Dear aunt! If I only would take her advice!
But I like my own way, and I find it so nice
And besides, I forget half the things I am told;
But they all will come back to me—when I am old.

If a youth passes by, it may happen, no doubt,
He may chance to look in as I chance to look out;
She would never endure an impertinent stare,—
It is horrid, she says, and I must n't sit there.

A walk in the moonlight has pleasures, I own,
But it is n't quite safe to be walking alone;
So I take a lad's arm,—just for safety, you know,—

But Aunt Tabitha tells me they did n't do so.

How wicked we are, and how good they were then!
They kept at arm's length those detestable men;
What an era of virtue she lived in!—But stay—
Were the men all such rogues in Aunt Tabitha's day?

If the men were so wicked, I 'll ask my papa
How he dared to propose to my darling mamma;
Was he like the rest of them? Goodness! Who knows?
And what shall I say, if a wretch should propose?

I am thinking if Aunt knew so little of sin,
What a wonder Aunt Tabitha's aunt must have been!
And her grand-aunt—it scares me—how shockingly sad
That we girls of to-day are so frightfully bad!

A martyr will save us, and nothing else can;
Let me perish—to rescue some wretched young man!
Though when to the altar a victim I go,
Aunt Tabitha 'll tell me she never did so.

WIND-CLOUDS AND STAR-DRIFTS

FROM THE YOUNG ASTRONOMER'S POEM

I.

AMBITION

ANOTHER clouded night; the stars are hid,
The orb that waits my search is hid with them.
Patience! Why grudge an hour, a month, a year,

To plant my ladder and to gain the round
That leads my footsteps to the heaven of fame,
Where waits the wreath my sleepless midnights won?
Not the stained laurel such as heroes wear
That withers when some stronger conqueror's heel
Treads down their shrivelling trophies in the dust;
But the fair garland whose undying green
Not time can change, nor wrath of gods or men!

With quickened heart-beats I shall hear tongues
That speak my praise; but better far the sense
That in the unshaped ages, buried deep
In the dark mines of unaccomplished time
Yet to be stamped with morning's royal die
And coined in golden days,—in those dim years
I shall be reckoned with the undying dead,
My name emblazoned on the fiery arch,
Unfading till the stars themselves shall fade.
Then, as they call the roll of shining worlds,
Sages of race unborn in accents new
Shall count me with the Olympian ones of old,
Whose glories kindle through the midnight sky
Here glows the God of Battles; this recalls
The Lord of Ocean, and yon far-off sphere
The Sire of Him who gave his ancient name
To the dim planet with the wondrous rings;
Here flames the Queen of Beauty's silver lamp,
And there the moon-girt orb of mighty Jove;
But this, unseen through all earth's ions past,
A youth who watched beneath the western star
Sought in the darkness, found, and shewed to men;
Linked with his name thenceforth and evermore
So shall that name be syllabled anew
In all the tongues of all the tribes of men:
I that have been through immemorial years
Dust in the dust of my forgotten time
Shall live in accents shaped of blood-warm breath,
Yea, rise in mortal semblance, newly born
In shining stone, in undecaying bronze,
And stand on high, and look serenely down
On the new race that calls the earth its own.

Is this a cloud, that, blown athwart my soul,

Wears a false seeming of the pearly stain
Where worlds beyond the world their mingling rays
Blend in soft white,—a cloud that, born of earth,
Would cheat the soul that looks for light from heaven?
Must every coral-insect leave his sign
On each poor grain he lent to build the reef,
As Babel's builders stamped their sunburnt clay,
Or deem his patient service all in vain?
What if another sit beneath the shade
Of the broad elm I planted by the way,—
What if another heed the beacon light
I set upon the rock that wrecked my keel,—
Have I not done my task and served my kind?
Nay, rather act thy part, unnamed, unknown,
And let Fame blow her trumpet through the world
With noisy wind to swell a fool's renown,
Joined with some truth he stumbled blindly o'er,
Or coupled with some single shining deed
That in the great account of all his days
Will stand alone upon the bankrupt sheet
His pitying angel shows the clerk of Heaven.
The noblest service comes from nameless hands,
And the best servant does his work unseen.
Who found the seeds of fire and made them shoot,
Fed by his breath, in buds and flowers of flame?
Who forged in roaring flames the ponderous stone,
And shaped the moulded metal to his need?
Who gave the dragging car its rolling wheel,
And tamed the steed that whirls its circling round?
All these have left their work and not their names,—
Why should I murmur at a fate like theirs?
This is the heavenly light; the pearly stain
Was but a wind-cloud drifting o'er the stars!

II.

REGRETS

BRIEF glimpses of the bright celestial spheres,
False lights, false shadows, vague, uncertain gleams,

Pale vaporous mists, wan streaks of lurid flame,
The climbing of the upward-sailing cloud,
The sinking of the downward-falling star,—
All these are pictures of the changing moods
Borne through the midnight stillness of my soul.

Here am I, bound upon this pillared rock,
Prey to the vulture of a vast desire
That feeds upon my life. I burst my bands
And steal a moment's freedom from the beak,
The clinging talons and the shadowing plumes;
Then comes the false enchantress, with her song;

"Thou wouldst not lay thy forehead in the dust
Like the base herd that feeds and breeds and dies
Lo, the fair garlands that I weave for thee,
Unchanging as the belt Orion wears,
Bright as the jewels of the seven-starred Crown,
The spangled stream of Berenice's hair!"
And so she twines the fetters with the flowers
Around my yielding limbs, and the fierce bird
Stoops to his quarry,—then to feed his rage
Of ravening hunger I must drain my blood
And let the dew-drenched, poison-breeding night
Steal all the freshness from my fading cheek,
And leave its shadows round my caverned eyes.
All for a line in some unheeded scroll;
All for a stone that tells to gaping clowns,
"Here lies a restless wretch beneath a clod
Where squats the jealous nightmare men call
Fame!"

I marvel not at him who scorns his kind
And thinks not sadly of the time foretold
When the old hulk we tread shall be a wreck,
A slag, a cinder drifting through the sky
Without its crew of fools! We live too long,
And even so are not content to die,
But load the mould that covers up our bones
With stones that stand like beggars by the road
And show death's grievous wound and ask for tears;
Write our great books to teach men who we are,
Sing our fine songs that tell in artful phrase

The secrets of our lives, and plead and pray
For alms of memory with the after time,
Those few swift seasons while the earth shall wear
Its leafy summers, ere its core grows cold
And the moist life of all that breathes shall die;
Or as the new-born seer, perchance more wise,
Would have us deem, before its growing mass,
Pelted with star-dust, stoned with meteor-balls,
Heats like a hammered anvil, till at last
Man and his works and all that stirred itself
Of its own motion, in the fiery glow
Turns to a flaming vapor, and our orb
Shines a new sun for earths that shall be born.

I am as old as Egypt to myself,
Brother to them that squared the pyramids
By the same stars I watch. I read the page
Where every letter is a glittering world,
With them who looked from Shinar's clay-built towers,
Ere yet the wanderer of the Midland sea
Had missed the fallen sister of the seven.
I dwell in spaces vague, remote, unknown,
Save to the silent few, who, leaving earth,
Quit all communion with their living time.
I lose myself in that ethereal void,
Till I have tired my wings and long to fill
My breast with denser air, to stand, to walk
With eyes not raised above my fellow-men.
Sick of my unwalled, solitary realm,
I ask to change the myriad lifeless worlds
I visit as mine own for one poor patch
Of this dull spheroid and a little breath
To shape in word or deed to serve my kind.
Was ever giant's dungeon dug so deep,
Was ever tyrant's fetter forged so strong,
Was e'er such deadly poison in the draught
The false wife mingles for the trusting fool,
As he whose willing victim is himself,
Digs, forges, mingles, for his captive soul?

III.

THE snows that glittered on the disk of Mars
Have melted, and the planet's fiery orb
Rolls in the crimson summer of its year;
But what to me the summer or the snow
Of worlds that throb with life in forms unknown,
If life indeed be theirs; I heed not these.
My heart is simply human; all my care
For them whose dust is fashioned like mine own;
These ache with cold and hunger, live in pain,
And shake with fear of worlds more full of woe;
There may be others worthier of my love,
But such I know not save through these I know.

There are two veils of language, hid beneath
Whose sheltering folds, we dare to be ourselves;
And not that other self which nods and smiles
And babbles in our name; the one is Prayer,
Lending its licensed freedom to the tongue
That tells our sorrows and our sins to Heaven;
The other, Verse, that throws its spangled web
Around our naked speech and makes it bold.
I, whose best prayer is silence; sitting dumb
In the great temple where I nightly serve
Him who is throned in light, have dared to claim
The poet's franchise, though I may not hope
To wear his garland; hear me while I tell
My story in such form as poets use,
But breathed in fitful whispers, as the wind
Sighs and then slumbers, wakes and sighs again.

Thou Vision, floating in the breathless air
Between me and the fairest of the stars,
I tell my lonely thoughts as unto thee.
Look not for marvels of the scholar's pen
In my rude measure; I can only show
A slender-margined, unillumined page,
And trust its meaning to the flattering eye
That reads it in the gracious light of love.
Ah, wouldst thou clothe thyself in breathing shape

And nestle at my side, my voice should lend
Whate'er my verse may lack of tender rhythm
To make thee listen.

    I have stood entranced
When, with her fingers wandering o'er the keys,
The white enchantress with the golden hair
Breathed all her soul through some unvalued rhyme;
Some flower of song that long had lost its bloom;
Lo! its dead summer kindled as she sang!
The sweet contralto, like the ringdove's coo,
Thrilled it with brooding, fond, caressing tones,
And the pale minstrel's passion lived again,
Tearful and trembling as a dewy rose
The wind has shaken till it fills the air
With light and fragrance. Such the wondrous charm
A song can borrow when the bosom throbs
That lends it breath.

    So from the poet's lips
His verse sounds doubly sweet, for none like him
Feels every cadence of its wave-like flow;
He lives the passion over, while he reads,
That shook him as he sang his lofty strain,
And pours his life through each resounding line,
As ocean, when the stormy winds are hushed,
Still rolls and thunders through his billowy caves.

IV.

MASTER AND SCHOLAR

LET me retrace the record of the years
That made me what I am. A man most wise,
But overworn with toil and bent with age,
Sought me to be his scholar,-me, run wild
From books and teachers,-kindled in my soul
The love of knowledge; led me to his tower,
Showed me the wonders of the midnight realm
His hollow sceptre ruled, or seemed to rule,
Taught me the mighty secrets of the spheres,
Trained me to find the glimmering specks of light

Beyond the unaided sense, and on my chart
To string them one by one, in order due,
As on a rosary a saint his beads.
I was his only scholar; I became
The echo to his thought; whate'er he knew
Was mine for asking; so from year to year
W e wrought together, till there came a time
When I, the learner, was the master half
Of the twinned being in the dome-crowned tower.

Minds roll in paths like planets; they revolve,
This in a larger, that a narrower ring,
But round they come at last to that same phase,
That selfsame light and shade they showed before.
I learned his annual and his monthly tale,
His weekly axiom and his daily phrase,
I felt them coming in the laden air,
And watched them laboring up to vocal breath,
Even as the first-born at his father's board
Knows ere he speaks the too familiar jest
Is on its way, by some mysterious sign
Forewarned, the click before the striking bell.

He shrivelled as I spread my growing leaves,
Till trust and reverence changed to pitying care;
He lived for me in what he once had been,
But I for him, a shadow, a defence,
The guardian of his fame, his guide, his staff,
Leaned on so long he fell if left alone.
I was his eye, his ear, his cunning hand,
Love was my spur and longing after fame,
But his the goading thorn of sleepless age
That sees its shortening span, its lengthening shades,
That clutches what it may with eager grasp,
And drops at last with empty, outstretched hands.
All this he dreamed not. He would sit him down
Thinking to work his problems as of old,
And find the star he thought so plain a blur,
The columned figures labyrinthine wilds
Without my comment, blind and senseless scrawls
That vexed him with their riddles; he would strive
And struggle for a while, and then his eye
Would lose its light, and over all his mind

The cold gray mist would settle; and erelong
The darkness fell, and I was left alone.

V.

ALONE

ALONE! no climber of an Alpine cliff,
No Arctic venturer on the waveless sea,
Feels the dread stillness round him as it chills
The heart of him who leaves the slumbering earth
To watch the silent worlds that crowd the sky.
Alone! And as the shepherd leaves his flock
To feed upon the hillside, he meanwhile
Finds converse in the warblings of the pipe
Himself has fashioned for his vacant hour,
So have I grown companion to myself,
And to the wandering spirits of the air
That smile and whisper round us in our dreams.
Thus have I learned to search if I may know
The whence and why of all beneath the stars
And all beyond them, and to weigh my life
As in a balance,—poising good and ill
Against each other,—asking of the Power
That flung me forth among the whirling worlds,
If I am heir to any inborn right,
Or only as an atom of the dust
That every wind may blow where'er it will.

VI.

QUESTIONING

I AM not humble; I was shown my place,
Clad in such robes as Nature had at hand;
Took what she gave, not chose; I know no shame,
No fear for being simply what I am.
I am not proud, I hold my every breath
At Nature's mercy. I am as a babe
Borne in a giant's arms, he knows not where;

Each several heart-beat, counted like the coin
A miser reckons, is a special gift
As from an unseen hand; if that withhold
Its bounty for a moment, I am left
A clod upon the earth to which I fall.

Something I find in me that well might claim
The love of beings in a sphere above
This doubtful twilight world of right and wrong;
Something that shows me of the self-same clay
That creeps or swims or flies in humblest form.
Had I been asked, before I left my bed
Of shapeless dust, what clothing I would wear,
I would have said, More angel and less worm;
But for their sake who are even such as I,
Of the same mingled blood, I would not choose
To hate that meaner portion of myself
Which makes me brother to the least of men.

I dare not be a coward with my lips
Who dare to question all things in my soul;
Some men may find their wisdom on their knees,
Some prone and grovelling in the dust like slaves;
Let the meek glowworm glisten in the dew;
I ask to lift my taper to the sky
As they who hold their lamps above their heads,
Trusting the larger currents up aloft,
Rather than crossing eddies round their breast,
Threatening with every puff the flickering blaze.

My life shall be a challenge, not a truce!
This is my homage to the mightier powers,
To ask my boldest question, undismayed
By muttered threats that some hysteric sense
Of wrong or insult will convulse the throne
Where wisdom reigns supreme; and if I err,
They all must err who have to feel their way
As bats that fly at noon; for what are we
But creatures of the night, dragged forth by day,
Who needs must stumble, and with stammering steps
Spell out their paths in syllables of pain?

Thou wilt not hold in scorn the child who dares
Look up to Thee, the Father,—dares to ask

More than thy wisdom answers. From thy hand
The worlds were cast; yet every leaflet claims
From that same hand its little shining sphere
Of star-lit dew; thine image, the great sun,
Girt with his mantle of tempestuous flame,
Glares in mid-heaven; but to his noon-tide blaze
The slender violet lifts its lidless eye,
And from his splendor steals its fairest hue,
Its sweetest perfume from his scorching fire.

VII.

WORSHIP

FROM my lone turret as I look around
O'er the green meadows to the ring of blue,
From slope, from summit, and from half-hid vale
The sky is stabbed with dagger-pointed spires,
Their gilded symbols whirling in the wind,
Their brazen tongues proclaiming to the world,
"Here truth is sold, the only genuine ware;
See that it has our trade-mark! You will buy
Poison instead of food across the way,
The lies of ———" this or that, each several name
The standard's blazon and the battle-cry
Of some true-gospel faction, and again
The token of the Beast to all beside.
And grouped round each I see a huddling crowd
Alike in all things save the words they use;
In love, in longing, hate and fear the same.

Whom do we trust and serve? We speak of one
And bow to many; Athens still would find
The shrines of all she worshipped safe within
Our tall barbarian temples, and the thrones
That crowned Olympus mighty as of old.
The god of music rules the Sabbath choir;
The lyric muse must leave the sacred nine
To help us please the dilettante's ear;
Plutus limps homeward with us, as we leave
The portals of the temple where we knelt
And listened while the god of eloquence

(Hermes of ancient days, but now disguised
In sable vestments) with that other god
Somnus, the son of Erebus and Nox,
Fights in unequal contest for our souls;
The dreadful sovereign of the underworld
Still shakes his sceptre at us, and we hear
The baying of the triple-throated hound;
Eros is young as ever, and as fair
The lovely Goddess born of ocean's foam.

These be thy gods, O Israel! Who is he,
The one ye name and tell us that ye serve,
Whom ye would call me from my lonely tower
To worship with the many-headed throng?
Is it the God that walked in Eden's grove
In the cool hour to seek our guilty sire?
The God who dealt with Abraham as the sons
Of that old patriarch deal with other men?
The jealous God of Moses, one who feels
An image as an insult, and is wroth
With him who made it and his child unborn?
The God who plagued his people for the sin
Of their adulterous king, beloved of him,—
The same who offers to a chosen few
The right to praise him in eternal song
While a vast shrieking world of endless woe
Blends its dread chorus with their rapturous hymn?
Is this the God ye mean, or is it he
Who heeds the sparrow's fall, whose loving heart
Is as the pitying father's to his child,
Whose lesson to his children is "Forgive,"
Whose plea for all, "They know not what they do"?

VIII.

MANHOOD

I CLAIM the right of knowing whom I serve,
Else is my service idle; He that asks
My homage asks it from a reasoning soul.
To crawl is not to worship; we have learned
A drill of eyelids, bended neck and knee,

Hanging our prayers on hinges, till we ape
The flexures of the many-jointed worm.
Asia has taught her Allahs and salaams
To the world's children,-we have grown to men!
We who have rolled the sphere beneath our feet
To find a virgin forest, as we lay
The beams of our rude temple, first of all
Must frame its doorway high enough for man
To pass unstooping; knowing as we do
That He who shaped us last of living forms
Has long enough been served by creeping things,
Reptiles that left their footprints in the sand
Of old sea-margins that have turned to stone,
And men who learned their ritual; we demand
To know Him first, then trust Him and then love
When we have found Him worthy of our love,
Tried by our own poor hearts and not before;
He must be truer than the truest friend,
He must be tenderer than a woman's love,
A father better than the best of sires;
Kinder than she who bore us, though we sin
Oftener than did the brother we are told We—
poor ill-tempered mortals—must forgive, Though
seven times sinning threescore times and ten.

This is the new world's gospel: Be ye men!
Try well the legends of the children's time;
Ye are the chosen people, God has led
Your steps across the desert of the deep
As now across the desert of the shore;
Mountains are cleft before you as the sea
Before the wandering tribe of Israel's sons;
Still onward rolls the thunderous caravan,
Its coming printed on the western sky,
A cloud by day, by night a pillared flame;
Your prophets are a hundred unto one
Of them of old who cried, "Thus saith the Lord;"
They told of cities that should fall in heaps,
But yours of mightier cities that shall rise
Where yet the lonely fishers spread their nets,
Where hides the fox and hoots the midnight owl;

The tree of knowledge in your garden grows
Not single, but at every humble door;
Its branches lend you their immortal food,
That fills you with the sense of what ye are,
No servants of an altar hewed and carved
From senseless stone by craft of human hands,
Rabbi, or dervish, brahmin, bishop, bonze,
But masters of the charm with which they work
To keep your hands from that forbidden tree!

Ye that have tasted that divinest fruit,
Look on this world of yours with opened eyes!
Y e are as gods! Nay, makers of your gods,—
Each day ye break an image in your shrine
And plant a fairer image where it stood
Where is the Moloch of your fathers' creed,
Whose fires of torment burned for span—long babes?
Fit object for a tender mother's love!
Why not? It was a bargain duly made
For these same infants through the surety's act
Intrusted with their all for earth and heaven,
By Him who chose their guardian, knowing well
His fitness for the task,—this, even this,
Was the true doctrine only yesterday
As thoughts are reckoned,—and to—day you hear
In words that sound as if from human tongues
Those monstrous, uncouth horrors of the past
That blot the blue of heaven and shame the earth
As would the saurians of the age of slime,
Awaking from their stony sepulchres
And wallowing hateful in the eye of day!

IX.

RIGHTS

WHAT am I but the creature Thou hast made?
What have I save the blessings Thou hast lent?
What hope I but thy mercy and thy love?
Who but myself shall cloud my soul with fear?
Whose hand protect me from myself but thine?
I claim the rights of weakness, I, the babe,

Call on my sire to shield me from the ills
That still beset my path, not trying me
With snares beyond my wisdom or my strength,
He knowing I shall use them to my harm,
And find a tenfold misery in the sense
That in my childlike folly I have sprung
The trap upon myself as vermin use,
Drawn by the cunning bait to certain doom.
Who wrought the wondrous charm that leads us on
To sweet perdition, but the selfsame power
That set the fearful engine to destroy
His wretched offspring (as the Rabbis tell),
And hid its yawning jaws and treacherous springs
In such a show of innocent sweet flowers
It lured the sinless angels and they fell?
Ah! He who prayed the prayer of all mankind
Summed in those few brief words the mightiest plea
For erring souls before the courts of heaven,—
Save us from being tempted,—lest we fall!

If we are only as the potter's clay
Made to be fashioned as the artist wills,
And broken into shards if we offend
The eye of Him who made us, it is well;
Such love as the insensate lump of clay
That spins upon the swift-revolving wheel
Bears to the hand that shapes its growing form,—
Such love, no more, will be our hearts' return
To the great Master-workman for his care,—
Or would be, save that this, our breathing clay,
Is intertwined with fine innumerous threads
That make it conscious in its framer's hand;
And this He must remember who has filled
These vessels with the deadly draught of life,—
Life, that means death to all it claims. Our love
Must kindle in the ray that streams from heaven,
A faint reflection of the light divine;
The sun must warm the earth before the rose
Can show her inmost heart-leaves to the sun.

He yields some fraction of the Maker's right
Who gives the quivering nerve its sense of pain;
Is there not something in the pleading eye

Of the poor brute that suffers, which arraigns
The law that bids it suffer? Has it not
A claim for some remembrance in the book
That fills its pages with the idle words
Spoken of men? Or is it only clay,
Bleeding and aching in the potter's hand,
Yet all his own to treat it as He will
And when He will to cast it at his feet,
Shattered, dishonored, lost forevermore?
My dog loves me, but could he look beyond
His earthly master, would his love extend
To Him who—Hush! I will not doubt that He
Is better than our fears, and will not wrong
The least, the meanest of created things!

He would not trust me with the smallest orb
That circles through the sky; He would not give
A meteor to my guidance; would not leave
The coloring of a cloudlet to my hand;
He locks my beating heart beneath its bars
And keeps the key himself; He measures out
The draughts of vital breath that warm my blood,
Winds up the springs of instinct which uncoil,
Each in its season; ties me to my home,
My race, my time, my nation, and my creed
So closely that if I but slip my wrist
Out of the band that cuts it to the bone,
Men say, "He hath a devil;" He has lent
All that I hold in trust, as unto one
By reason of his weakness and his years
Not fit to hold the smallest shred in fee
Of those most common things he calls his own,—
And yet—my Rabbi tells me—He has left
The care of that to which a million worlds
Filled with unconscious life were less than naught,
Has left that mighty universe, the Soul,
To the weak guidance of our baby hands,
Let the foul fiends have access at their will,
Taking the shape of angels, to our hearts,—
Our hearts already poisoned through and through
With the fierce virus of ancestral sin;
Turned us adrift with our immortal charge,

To wreck ourselves in gulfs of endless woe.

If what my Rabbi tells me is the truth
Why did the choir of angels sing for joy?
Heaven must be compassed in a narrow space,
And offer more than room enough for all
That pass its portals; but the under-world,
The godless realm, the place where demons forge
Their fiery darts and adamantine chains,
Must swarm with ghosts that for a little while
Had worn the garb of flesh, and being heirs
Of all the dulness of their stolid sires,
And all the erring instincts of their tribe,
Nature's own teaching, rudiments of "sin,"
Fell headlong in the snare that could not fail
To trap the wretched creatures shaped of clay
And cursed with sense enough to lose their souls!

Brother, thy heart is troubled at my word;
Sister, I see the cloud is on thy brow.
He will not blame me, He who sends not peace,
But sends a sword, and bids us strike amain
At Error's gilded crest, where in the van
Of earth's great army, mingling with the best
And bravest of its leaders, shouting loud
The battle-cries that yesterday have led
The host of Truth to victory, but to-day
Are watchwords of the laggard and the slave,
He leads his dazzled cohorts. God has made
This world a strife of atoms and of spheres;
With every breath I sigh myself away
And take my tribute from the wandering wind
To fan the flame of life's consuming fire;
So, while my thought has life, it needs must burn,
And, burning, set the stubble-fields ablaze,
Where all the harvest long ago was reaped
And safely garnered in the ancient barns.
But still the gleaners, groping for their food,
Go blindly feeling through the close-shorn straw,
While the young reapers flash, their glittering steel
Where later suns have ripened nobler grain!

X.

THE time is racked with birth-pangs; every hour
Brings forth some gasping truth, and truth newborn
Looks a misshapen and untimely growth,
The terror of the household and its shame,
A monster coiling in its nurse's lap
That some would strangle, some would only starve;
But still it breathes, and passed from hand to hand,
And suckled at a hundred half-clad breasts,
Comes slowly to its stature and its form,
Calms the rough ridges of its dragon-scales,
Changes to shining locks its snaky hair,
And moves transfigured into angel guise,
Welcomed by all that cursed its hour of birth,
And folded in the same encircling arms
That cast it like a serpent from their hold!

If thou wouldst live in honor, die in peace,
Have the fine words the marble-workers learn
To carve so well, upon thy funeral-stone,
And earn a fair obituary, dressed
In all the many-colored robes of praise,
Be deafer than the adder to the cry
Of that same foundling truth, until it grows
To seemly favor, and at length has won
The smiles of hard-mouthed men and light-lipped dames;
Then snatch it from its meagre nurse's breast,
Fold it in silk and give it food from gold;
So shalt thou share its glory when at last
It drops its mortal vesture, and, revealed
In all the splendor of its heavenly form,
Spreads on the startled air its mighty wings!

Alas! how much that seemed immortal truth
That heroes fought for, martyrs died to save,
Reveals its earth-born lineage, growing old
And limping in its march, its wings unplumed,
Its heavenly semblance faded like a dream!
Here in this painted casket, just unsealed,
Lies what was once a breathing shape like thine,

Once loved as thou art loved; there beamed the eyes
That looked on Memphis in its hour of pride,
That saw the walls of hundred-gated Thebes,
And all the mirrored glories of the Nile.
See how they toiled that all-consuming time
Might leave the frame immortal in its tomb;
Filled it with fragrant balms and odorous gums
That still diffuse their sweetness through the air,
And wound and wound with patient fold on fold
The flaxen bands thy hand has rudely torn!
Perchance thou yet canst see the faded stain
Of the sad mourner's tear.

XI.

IDOLS

BUT what is this?
The sacred beetle, bound upon the breast
Of the blind heathen! Snatch the curious prize,
Give it a place among thy treasured spoils,
Fossil and relic,—corals, encrinites,
The fly in amber and the fish in stone,
The twisted circlet of Etruscan gold,
Medal, intaglio, poniard, poison-ring,—
Place for the Memphian beetle with thine hoard!

AM longer than thy creed has blest the world
This toy, thus ravished from thy brother's breast,
Was to the heart of Mizraim as divine,
As holy, as the symbol that we lay
On the still bosom of our white-robed dead,
And raise above their dust that all may know
Here sleeps an heir of glory. Loving friends,
With tears of trembling faith and choking sobs,
And prayers to those who judge of mortal deeds,
Wrapped this poor image in the cerement's fold
That Isis and Osiris, friends of man,
Might know their own and claim the ransomed soul.

An idol? Man was born to worship such!
An idol is an image of his thought;

Sometimes he carves it out of gleaming stone,
And sometimes moulds it out of glittering gold,
Or rounds it in a mighty frescoed dome,
Or lifts it heavenward in a lofty spire,
Or shapes it in a cunning frame of words,
Or pays his priest to make it day by day;
For sense must have its god as well as soul;
A new-born Dian calls for silver shrines,
And Egypt's holiest symbol is our own,
The sign we worship as did they of old
When Isis and Osiris ruled the world.

Let us be true to our most subtle selves,
We long to have our idols like the rest.
Think! when the men of Israel had their God
Encamped among them, talking with their chief,
Leading them in the pillar of the cloud
And watching o'er them in the shaft of fire,
They still must have an image; still they longed
For somewhat of substantial, solid form
Whereon to hang their garlands, and to fix
Their wandering thoughts and gain a stronger hold
For their uncertain faith, not yet assured
If those same meteors of the day and night
Were not mere exhalations of the soil.
Are we less earthly than the chosen race?
Are we more neighbors of the living God
Than they who gathered manna every morn,
Reaping where none had sown, and heard the voice
Of him who met the Highest in the mount,
And brought them tables, graven with His hand?
Yet these must have their idol, brought their gold,
That star-browed Apis might be god again;
Yea, from their ears the women brake the rings
That lent such splendors to the gypsy brown
Of sunburnt cheeks,—what more could woman do
To show her pious zeal? They went astray,
But nature led them as it leads us all.
We too, who mock at Israel's golden calf
And scoff at Egypt's sacred scarabee,
Would have our amulets to clasp and kiss,
And flood with rapturous tears, and bear with us

To be our dear companions in the dust;
Such magic works an image in our souls.

Man is an embryo; see at twenty years
His bones, the columns that uphold his frame
Not yet cemented, shaft and capital,
Mere fragments of the temple incomplete.
At twoscore, threescore, is he then full grown?
Nay, still a child, and as the little maids
Dress and undress their puppets, so he tries
To dress a lifeless creed, as if it lived,
And change its raiment when the world cries shame!

We smile to see our little ones at play
So grave, so thoughtful, with maternal care
Nursing the wisps of rags they call their babes;—
Does He not smile who sees us with the toys
We call by sacred names, and idly feign
To be what we have called them? He is still
The Father of this helpless nursery-brood,
Whose second childhood joins so close its first,
That in the crowding, hurrying years between
We scarce have trained our senses to their task
Before the gathering mist has dimmed our eyes,
And with our hollowed palm we help our ear,
And trace with trembling hand our wrinkled names,
And then begin to tell our stories o'er,
And see—not hear—the whispering lips that say,
"You know? Your father knew him.—This is he,
Tottering and leaning on the hireling's arm,"—
And so, at length, disrobed of all that clad
The simple life we share with weed and worm,
Go to our cradles, naked as we came.

XII.

LOVE

WHAT if a soul redeemed, a spirit that loved
While yet on earth and was beloved in turn,
And still remembered every look and tone
Of that dear earthly sister who was left

Among the unwise virgins at the gate,—
Itself admitted with the bridegroom's train,—
What if this spirit redeemed, amid the host
Of chanting angels, in some transient lull
Of the eternal anthem, heard the cry
Of its lost darling, whom in evil hour
Some wilder pulse of nature led astray
And left an outcast in a world of fire,
Condemned to be the sport of cruel fiends,
Sleepless, unpitying, masters of the skill
To wring the maddest ecstasies of pain
From worn-out souls that only ask to die,—
Would it not long to leave the bliss of heaven,—
Bearing a little water in its hand
To moisten those poor lips that plead in vain
With Him we call our Father? Or is all
So changed in such as taste celestial joy
They hear unmoved the endless wail of woe;
The daughter in the same dear tones that hushed
Her cradle slumbers; she who once had held
A babe upon her bosom from its voice
Hoarse with its cry of anguish, yet the same?

No! not in ages when the Dreadful Bird
Stamped his huge footprints, and the Fearful Beast
Strode with the flesh about those fossil bones
We build to mimic life with pygmy hands,—
Not in those earliest days when men ran wild
And gashed each other with their knives of stone,
When their low foreheads bulged in ridgy brows
And their flat hands were callous in the palm
With walking in the fashion of their sires,
Grope as they might to find a cruel god
To work their will on such as human wrath
Had wrought its worst to torture, and had left
With rage unsated, white and stark and cold,
Could hate have shaped a demon more malign
Than him the dead men mummied in their creed
And taught their trembling children to adore!

Made in his image! Sweet and gracious souls
Dear to my heart by nature's fondest names,
Is not your memory still the precious mould

That lends its form to Him who hears my prayer?
Thus only I behold Him, like to them,
Long-suffering, gentle, ever slow to wrath,
If wrath it be that only wounds to heal,
Ready to meet the wanderer ere he reach
The door he seeks, forgetful of his sin,
Longing to clasp him in a father's arms,
And seal his pardon with a pitying tear!

Four gospels tell their story to mankind,
And none so full of soft, caressing words
That bring the Maid of Bethlehem and her Babe
Before our tear-dimmed eyes, as his who learned
In the meek service of his gracious art
The tones which, like the medicinal balms
That calm the sufferer's anguish, soothe our souls.
Oh that the loving woman, she who sat
So long a listener at her Master's feet,
Had left us Mary's Gospel,—all she heard
Too sweet, too subtle for the ear of man!
Mark how the tender-hearted mothers read
The messages of love between the lines
Of the same page that loads the bitter tongue
Of him who deals in terror as his trade
With threatening words of wrath that scorch like flame
They tell of angels whispering round the bed
Of the sweet infant smiling in its dream,
Of lambs enfolded in the Shepherd's arms,
Of Him who blessed the children; of the land
Where crystal rivers feed unfading flowers,
Of cities golden-paved with streets of pearl,
Of the white robes the winged creatures wear,
The crowns and harps from whose melodious strings
One long, sweet anthem flows forevermore!
We too had human mothers, even as Thou,
Whom we have learned to worship as remote
From mortal kindred, wast a cradled babe.
The milk of woman filled our branching veins,
She lulled us with her tender nursery-song,
And folded round us her untiring arms,
While the first unremembered twilight yeas
Shaped us to conscious being; still we feel

Her pulses in our own,—too faintly feel;
Would that the heart of woman warmed our creeds!

Not from the sad-eyed hermit's lonely cell,
Not from the conclave where the holymen
Glare on each other, as with angry eyes
They battle for God's glory and their own,
Till, sick of wordy strife, a show of hands
Fixes the faith of ages yet unborn,—
Ah, not from these the listening soul can hear
The Father's voice that speaks itself divine!
Love must be still our Master; till we learn
What he can teach us of a woman's heart,
We know not His whose love embraces all.

EPILOGUE TO THE BREAKFAST-TABLE SERIES AUTOCRAT-PROFESSOR-POET

AT A BOOKSTORE

Anno Domini 1972

A CRAZY bookcase, placed before
A low-price dealer's open door;
Therein arrayed in broken rows
A ragged crew of rhyme and prose,
The homeless vagrants, waifs, and strays
Whose low estate this line betrays
(Set forth the lesser birds to lime)
YOUR CHOICE AMONG THESE BOORS 1 DIME!

Ho! dealer; for its motto's sake
This scarecrow from the shelf I take;
Three starveling volumes bound in one,
Its covers warping in the sun.
Methinks it hath a musty smell,
I like its flavor none too well,
But Yorick's brain was far from dull,
Though Hamlet pah!'d, and dropped his skull.

Why, here comes rain! The sky grows dark,—
Was that the roll of thunder? Hark!
The shop affords a safe retreat,
A chair extends its welcome seat,
The tradesman has a civil look
(I 've paid, impromptu, for my book),
The clouds portend a sudden shower,—
I 'll read my purchase for an hour.

What have I rescued from the shelf?
A Boswell, writing out himself!
For though he changes dress and name,
The man beneath is still the same,
Laughing or sad, by fits and starts,
One actor in a dozen parts,

And whatsoe'er the mask may be,
The voice assures us, This is he.

I say not this to cry him down;
I find my Shakespeare in his clown,
His rogues the selfsame parent own;
Nay! Satan talks in Milton's tone!
Where'er the ocean inlet strays,
The salt sea wave its source betrays;
Where'er the queen of summer blows,
She tells the zephyr, "I'm the rose!"

And his is not the playwright's page;
His table does not ape the stage;
What matter if the figures seen
Are only shadows on a screen,
He finds in them his lurking thought,
And on their lips the words he sought,
Like one who sits before the keys
And plays a tune himself to please.

And was he noted in his day?
Read, flattered, honored? Who shall say?
Poor wreck of time the wave has cast
To find a peaceful shore at last,
Once glorying in thy gilded name
And freighted deep with hopes of fame,
Thy leaf is moistened with a tear,
The first for many a long, long year.

For be it more or less of art
That veils the lowliest human heart
Where passion throbs, where friendship glows,
Where pity's tender tribute flows,
Where love has lit its fragrant fire,
And sorrow quenched its vain desire,
For me the altar is divine,
Its flame, its ashes,—all are mine!

And thou, my brother, as I look
And see thee pictured in thy book,
Thy years on every page confessed
In shadows lengthening from the west,
Thy glance that wanders, as it sought
Some freshly opening flower of thought,

Thy hopeful nature, light and free,
I start to find myself in thee!

… … … . .

Come, vagrant, outcast, wretch forlorn
In leather jerkin stained and torn,
Whose talk has filled my idle hour
And made me half forget the shower,
I'll do at least as much for you,
Your coat I'll patch, your gilt renew,
Read you—perhaps—some other time.
Not bad, my bargain! Price one dime!

CPSIA information can be obtained
at www.ICGtesting.com
Printed in the USA
LVHW040445060820
662304LV00008B/1798

9 783752 303070